Itsy-Bitsy
Giant

Written by Melanie Martin
Illustrated by Doug Cushman

Troll Associates

Library of Congress Cataloging-in-Publication Data

Martin, Melanie.
    Itsy-bitsy giant / written by Melanie Martin; illustrated by
Doug Cushman.
        p.   cm.—(Fiddlesticks)
    Summary: Gilbert the giant,thinks it's fun to frighten people,
until a magician makes him itsy-bitsy and he finds out what it's
like to be smaller than everyone else.
    ISBN 0-8167-1335-9 (lib. bdg.)   ISBN 0-8167-1336-7 (pbk.)
    [1. Giants—Fiction.   2. Size—Fiction.]   I. Cushman, Doug, ill.
II. Title.   III. Series.
PZ7.M36412It   1989
[E]—dc19   88-1234

Gilbert was taller than the tallest tree and
heavier than a mountain. Gilbert was a
giant—and not a very nice one at that.
Because he was big and strong, Gilbert
thought he could do anything he wanted.
He didn't care about anyone smaller than
himself. All he cared about was having fun.
And what was fun for Gilbert was not fun
for anyone else!

Gilbert thought it was fun to frighten
people. He really didn't want to hurt anyone,
but he liked to use his size to scare others.

Every time Gilbert approached a town, he
did the same awful thing. He stamped his
feet very hard. The ground trembled and
shook. Buildings rattled and quivered.
People ran out in alarm.

"What is it?" shouted the baker.

"What's happening?" cried the blacksmith.

"Why is everything shaking?" asked Timothy, the mayor's son.

"It must be an earthquake," yelled the mayor.

"It's not an earthquake," roared the giant, as he walked toward the town. "It's me, Gilbert the Giant. Run! Run or I'll step on you."

"Run for your lives!" cried the mayor.

"HO! HO! HO!" Gilbert chuckled, as he thundered into town. "Look at them go! What a funny sight!"

Gilbert stopped and watched as the people scrambled away. "Now I'll have some more fun," he said. Gilbert took a deep breath. He bent over and blew hard.

WHOOSH!

The giant's breath was as strong as a hurricane. People went tumbling toes over noses. Around and around they spun.

"HA! HA! HA!" laughed Gilbert. "This is fun!"

When the big wind finally stopped, the people staggered to their feet. Where could they go to escape the giant?

"Quick, everyone into that cave," shouted the mayor. "The giant won't be able to get us in there."

The people ran into the cave.

"The little mice scooted into a hole,"
laughed Gilbert. He bent down and peeked
into the cave. "Come out, little mice. I'm
staying here until you do."

Gilbert sat down near the mountain to
wait.

The day passed slowly. At long last, the mayor got up enough courage to peek outside.

"Please let us go home," he called to the giant. "We're all hot and hungry."

The giant smiled at the little man. "Hungry and hot?" mumbled Gilbert, as he stroked his chin thoughtfully. "I'll fix that. I'm really not a mean giant. I'll show you. I'll get food for everyone."

"Thank you," said the mayor. "What a nice thing to do."

Gilbert stood up. Two giant steps took him to a nearby farm. In a field was a crop of tomatoes. He scooped up a big bunch of plump, ripe tomatoes in his huge hands. "Soft, gushy tomatoes will be perfect," he chuckled, as he went back to the cave.

"Come out, little people," called Gilbert
as he stood above the cave. "Come out.
Lunch is served."

The people slowly came out. They eyed
the giant cautiously. He didn't look mean
anymore. In fact, he looked rather jolly.
He was grinning from ear to ear.

Everyone smiled up at Gilbert. Then,
suddenly, they saw something that made
them shudder.

"Oh no!" groaned the mayor. "What a
mean trick to play!"

Gilbert laughed and opened his hands.
It began to rain tomatoes.

SPLAT! WHUMP! PLOP! Ripe, gushy
tomatoes flew through the air. They dropped
and plopped here and there. Tomatoes
splattered all over the people below.

"Hot and hungry, you said," laughed
Gilbert. "Now I'll get some water to cool you
off."

The nasty giant bounded over to the river.
Cupping his hands, he dipped them into the
water. Then he threw the water at the crowd
near the cave.

SPLASH!

The downpour was terrible! Everyone
ended up sticky, soggy, and sloppy.

"HEH! HEH! HEH!" Gilbert laughed.
"This is the most fun I've had in a long
time." Away he walked, chuckling to himself.

The people grumbled angrily as the giant walked away. "I wish I was bigger than that giant," said the blacksmith. "I'd teach him a lesson."

"It would take magic to make you bigger than a giant," replied the baker.

"And the only one who can work magic is a magician," said Timothy.

Little did Gilbert realize that the stranger
he saw sitting in the forest was no ordinary
man. He was really a magician.

"What an odd-looking fellow," said
Gilbert as he studied the man's long, dark
robe and his tall, pointed cap. "I'll have some
fun with him."

BOOM! THUMP! STOMP!

Gilbert's footsteps echoed through the woods as he approached the strange little man. But the man never stirred. He sat silently on a hollow log and paid no attention to the giant.

"HEY, YOU!" thundered Gilbert. "Why don't you run away? Aren't you afraid of me?"

The strange man looked up at the giant.
"Why should I be afraid?" he asked calmly.

"Why? Why? Because I'm so BIG!"
Gilbert roared. Then he raised a huge foot
and held it above the man. "You are nothing
but an ant to me. I could squash you if I
wanted to."

Suddenly, the stranger leaped to his feet. "How dare you threaten Marvelo the Magician," said the man. He lifted his arm and pointed a finger at the giant. On that finger was Marvelo's magic ring.

"You called me an ant," Marvelo shouted.

Gilbert gulped nervously and lowered his foot to the ground.

"Perhaps you would be more mannerly if *you* were the size of an ant," said the magician.

Marvelo made a magic sign with his hand. His ring began to glow a bright red color. "*Abracadabra!*" said the magician.

POOF!

There was a blinding flash. Clouds of
thick smoke swirled around the giant.
Lightning crackled.

"What's happening to me?" cried Gilbert.

The giant had begun to shrink! He got
smaller and smaller. Down, down, down he
went. Soon Gilbert was no bigger than
a bug.

Marvelo smiled and bent over to look at
Gilbert. "Good-bye, my itsy-bitsy giant," said
the magician. "Now you will see what it's
like to be small."

"Wait, please!" shouted the itsy-bitsy
giant. "Don't leave me like this."

Marvelo didn't wait. He turned and
walked off into the woods.

BOOM! STOMP! THUMP!

The magician's footsteps were so loud,
Gilbert had to cover his ears with his hands.

"What an awful noise," complained the
itsy-bitsy giant. And for the first time he
knew what his own footsteps sounded like to
others.

Gilbert sat down on a twig to think. What should he do? He was worried and confused. He was used to everything looking small. Now everything looked so big. Flowers were as big as trees. Pebbles looked like boulders. "What a terrible fix I'm in," sighed the itsy-bitsy giant.

Gilbert scratched his head thoughtfully.
He needed help. "Maybe someone in town
can help me," he said. "But how can I get to
town? It would take days for someone so
small to walk that far."

Suddenly, a big grasshopper bounded out of the grass. Gilbert was so startled, he fell over backwards. As he lay there looking at the grasshopper, he got an idea.

Quietly, Gilbert sneaked up behind the grasshopper. The bug was so busy nibbling on a tasty leaf it didn't even notice him. Closer, closer, closer crept Gilbert.

"Now!" he shouted as he leaped on the grasshopper's back.

BOING! BOING! BOING! Away went the grasshopper. Away went the itsy-bitsy giant. BOING! BOING! BOING! The bounding bug sped down the road that led to town.

"This isn't the easiest way to travel," groaned Gilbert, as he hung on tightly. "But at least it's fast."

A short time later, Gilbert and the grasshopper reached the town. The bug suddenly halted right in the middle of the road.

"I guess it's time to get off," said Gilbert, as he relaxed his grip.

Just then the grasshopper kicked hard and sprung high into the air.

"WHOA!" yelled Gilbert, as he sailed off the bug's back.

THUD!

The itsy-bitsy giant landed flat on his face in the dirt. The bug looked back at Gilbert and then bounded away.

Gilbert was still sprawled in the dust
when he heard a horrible sound. BOOM!
THUMP! STOMP! BOOM! The itsy-bitsy
giant looked up.

A group of children were playing tag.
They were running right at him. If he didn't
move and move fast, the ant-sized giant
would be squashed.

Gilbert scrambled to his feet. Where could
he go? He glanced around looking for a safe
spot. He spied the blacksmith's shop. In the
wall was a small mouse hole. The itsy-bitsy
giant ran for his life.

BOOM! THUMP! STOMP! STOMP!

The feet came closer. *Zip!* Gilbert scooted
into the mouse hole just as the children
thundered past.

"Phew!" sighed Gilbert. "That was awful.
Seeing those big feet above me was really
frightening. I could have been mashed like a
potato."

Then it dawned on Gilbert that he had
once frightened people in that very same
way. Gilbert shook his head and started
toward the other end of the mouse hole.
There the blacksmith was working in his shop.

The itsy-bitsy giant peeked out of his hole. The blacksmith was near the fire. He was using bellows to fan the fire. Bellows shoot air out in big gusts.

Gilbert decided to take a chance and ask the blacksmith for help. He stepped out of the mouse hole and started across the floor.

"Hey! Hey, you!" yelled Gilbert, as loudly as he could. The blacksmith stopped and looked around. He didn't see anyone, so he shrugged his shoulders and went back to work.

"Hey!" screamed Gilbert. "I'm down here!"

This time the blacksmith spotted Gilbert
on the floor. But he didn't know it was an
itsy-bitsy giant.

"A bug! A big, ugly one!" groaned the
blacksmith. "I hate bugs!"

He aimed the bellows at Gilbert and
squeezed it tightly. WHOOSH! Out came a
blast of air. Down went Gilbert. Over and
over he rolled, head over heels. He tumbled
back into the mouse hole and then out of the
mouse hole and back into the street.

The dizzy, itsy-bitsy giant struggled to his
feet. Slowly, he staggered past the baker's
house. Suddenly, the baker came out.
She was holding a bucket of dirty dishwater.
She tossed the water into the street.

SPLASH!

"Yipes!" yelled Gilbert, as the water washed him away. Down the street he floated in a flood of soapy bubbles.

Finally, the water began to seep into the ground. The itsy-bitsy giant was left in a pool of icky-sticky mud. Gilbert was trapped and sinking fast. The more he struggled to free himself, the deeper he sank.

"Help!" called Gilbert. "Someone help me."

But Gilbert was so tiny, he was hard to
see. People walked by as he struggled in the
mud. Just when Gilbert was about to give
up, little Timothy walked by. As Timothy
passed the patch of mud, something caught
his eye.

"Some poor little thing is trapped," said the boy. "I'll help it." Timothy bent down to take a closer look.

"Help me, please!" Gilbert shouted.

Timothy was surprised at what he saw. "It's not a bug," said the boy. "It's . . . it's the mean giant. But now he's an itsy-bitsy giant."

Gilbert sighed in dismay. The boy had
recognized him. Gilbert was certain Timothy
would not help him after all the nasty things
he'd done. But Gilbert was wrong.

"Big people should always help little
people," Timothy said, as he carefully lifted
Gilbert out of the mud.

"Thank you," said Gilbert, as he stood up in the boy's hand. "If I ever get big again, I'll remember what you just said."

The boy smiled at the itsy-bitsy giant. "How did you get so small?" Timothy asked.

Gilbert told the boy about Marvelo the Magician. Timothy offered to help Gilbert. Together they went off to search for Marvelo.

Timothy and Gilbert looked here and there. They searched everywhere for Marvelo the Magician. At long last, they came upon the magical little man. He was sitting near a huge patch of thick, prickly thorn bushes. He looked upset.

"What do you want, lad?" asked Marvelo when he saw Timothy.

Timothy held out his hand. Sitting in it was Gilbert. "I'd like you to change this itsy-bitsy giant back into a giant-sized giant," said Timothy.

"Please change me back," begged Gilbert. "I've learned my lesson. I'll never use my size to frighten anyone ever again. I'll only use it to help people."

"You seem to have learned your lesson,"
said Marvelo. "And I would change you back
if I could, but to work magic I need my
magic ring."

"Where is your ring?" asked Timothy.

Marvelo pointed at the thorn bushes.
"I took it off to polish it," Marvelo explained.
"I accidentally dropped it. The ring rolled
deep into the thorns where no one can reach
it."

Timothy looked at the bushes. The vines were thick and snarled. The huge thorns on them were very sharp.

"I can get the ring!" shouted Gilbert. "I'm so small I can slip past the thorns without getting hurt. Put me down, Timothy."

Timothy placed Gilbert on the ground.
The itsy-bitsy giant carefully squeezed
through the tiny spaces between the thorns.
Soon he was out of sight.

"That giant certainly has changed,"
Marvelo said to Timothy.

Timothy nodded. "Now he knows big
people should always help little people."

"And little people should help big people," shouted Gilbert, as he popped out of the bushes. He smiled and held up Marvelo's magic ring.

"My ring!" shouted the magician happily, slipping it on his finger. "Now I can change you back to your rightful size."

Marvelo's magic ring began to glow.
"*Abracadabra!*" shouted the magician.
There was a bright flash.

POOF!

Gilbert began to grow. He grew and
grew, until he was once again a giant.

"Thank you both very much," said Gilbert
to Marvelo and Timothy. The magician and
the boy smiled at the giant.

From that day on, Gilbert was a good giant. He never scared anyone smaller than himself, and he used his giant size only to help others.

"Big or small, we all should help each other," Gilbert the Giant often said to his friends.